Who Will Play With Me?

For Anna Bootle

Also by Michèle Coxon

The Cat who Lost his Purr
The Cat who Found his Way Home
Catch Up, Little Cheetah!
Helpful Puppy!
It's Mine!
Kitten's Adventure
Kitten Finds a Home
Look Out, Lion Cub!
Naughty Kitten!
Too Big!
Where's My Kitten?

Who Will Play With Me?

Michèle Coxon

Happy Cat Books

Pumpkin had a lovely home.
She had a warm soft bed and
plenty of toys. But she was lonely.
"Who will play with me?"

Luke had a lovely home, too.
He had games and books and a
friendly teddy bear. But he had no
one to share them with.

"Will you play with me?" Pumpkin meowed to Captain.
"No," yawned the old cat.
"I want to sleep and dream of fish."

"Play with me!" Luke whispered to Ben.

"No," the old dog yawned, "I want to sleep and dream of bones."

"Can I climb up?" asked Pumpkin.
"Ouch!" the lady cried, "I'm busy,
go and play."

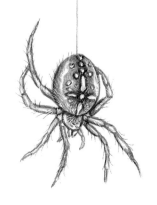

"Shall we play a game?"
Luke asked his mum.
"Not now," she replied.
"I'm busy, go and play
outside."

"Let's play together!" meowed
Pumpkin to the birds.
"No thanks," they chirped as they
flew away.

"Shall we play a game?" Luke asked a frog.
"No," croaked the frog. "I'm looking for food."

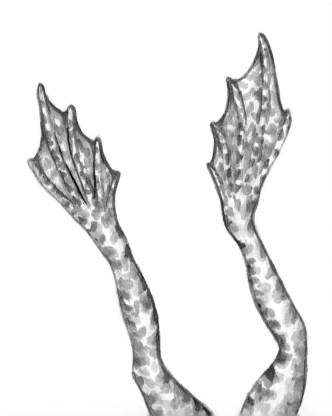

Pumpkin crawled bravely through the jungle of grass.

Luke crept silently through the
overgrown garden.

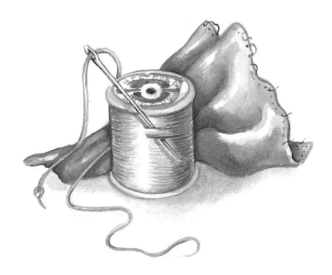

What should Pumpkin find but a funny creature with two big green eyes and a furry head.

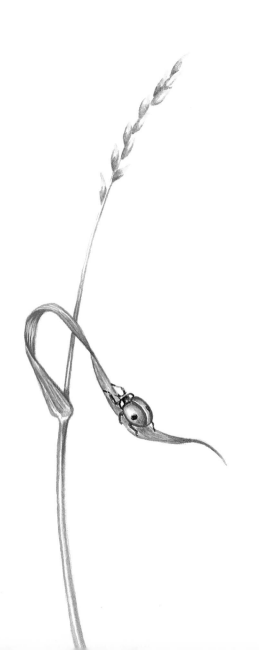

What should Luke find but a funny
creature with two big green eyes
and a furry face.

Then they both asked each
other the same question at
the same time.

"WILL YOU PLAY WITH ME?"

HAPPY CAT BOOKS

Published by Happy Cat Books Ltd.
Bradfield, Essex CO11 2UT, UK

This edition published 2002
1 3 5 7 9 10 8 6 4 2

A CIP catalogue record for this book is available from the British Library

ISBN 1 903285 15 1 Paperback

Printed in Hong Kong by Wing King Tong Co. Ltd.